Goose
in a hole

Judith Kerr

HarperCollins *Children's Books*

For my dear

granddaughter

Tatiana

with love

First published in Great Britain by HarperCollins Children's Books in 2005

1 3 5 7 9 10 8 6 4 2
ISBN: 0 00 720793 X

HarperCollins Children's Books is a division of HarperCollins Publishers Ltd.
Text and illustrations copyright © Kerr-Kneale Productions Ltd 2005
The author/illustrator asserts the moral right to be identified as the author/illustrator of the work.
A CIP catalogue record for this title is available from the British Library.

Visit our website at: www.harpercollinschildrensbooks.co.uk

Printed and bound in China

One night Katerina suddenly woke up.
Something was wrong in her pond.
"Where's all the water?" said Katerina.

"It's running down a big hole," said Charlie.
"Well, run after it, quick!" said Katerina.
"It must be going to a new pond somewhere else."
So Charlie ran after the water,
and Katerina ran after Charlie,
and the goslings ran after Katerina,
down the big hole.

In the morning everyone was very surprised
to see what happened to the pond.
"Where's all the water?" said Bert from the fruit shop.
"And where's Katerina?" said Millie Buswell.

"It must have gone down that big hole,"
said Miss Jones who taught dancing.
"I will speak to my husband," said Mrs Patel
from the paper shop. "He is very wise
about the ways of water."

Mr Patel was talking to the mayor.
He was putting a new bath in the mayor's bathroom.
"Never mind about my bath," said the mayor.
"We must go at once to look at this hole in the pond."

"Oh my goodness," said Mr Patel.
"Something must have given way.
The pipes will be all ajumble underground."
"Well, we must get our pond back," said the mayor.
"And we must find Katerina," said Millie.
"I'm worried about her. Wherever can she be?"

Katerina, Charlie and the goslings were in the big hole underground.
The hole went up and down and up and down and on and on and on.
"Which is the way to the new pond?" said Charlie.
"I'll know it when I see it," said Katerina.

After a while she saw it.
"This is it," said Katerina.
"This will lead us to a lovely new pond."
BUT…

"This is not lovely and it is not a pond," said Charlie. "There isn't even any water."
"All right, try again," said Katerina.
"But I'm sure we'll find a lovely new pond quite soon."

Back at the old pond Mr Patel had covered up the hole.
"Please can we go and look for Katerina?" said Millie.
"Later," said Mr Patel. "First we must fill the pond with water."

"Later," said Miss Jones. "I'm afraid this will take some time."

"Later," said the mayor.
"Mrs Patel has had a very good idea."

"Later," said Mrs Patel. "Mr Patel's brother is coming to help.
He is widely known to be very speedy with water…

…and here he is. Now we shall soon be done."

"And then we can go and look for Katerina?" said Millie.

"Of course," said Mrs Patel. "Of course," said Mr Patel.

"Of course," said Miss Jones. "Of course," said the mayor.

"Just as soon as we've filled up the pond."

"I'm worried about her," said Millie.

"Where can she have got to?"

Katerina had found another way out of the hole.
"This really is it," she said.

"I'm sure this will take us to a lovely new pond with
lots of water."
BUT…

"This pond has too much water and
it is all in the wrong place," said Charlie.
"It is the wrong sort of water."
"Oh, all right, try again," said Katerina.
"But I'm sure we'll find a lovely new pond quite soon."

Back at Katerina's old pond everyone was tired
after filling it up with water.
"NOW!" said Millie. "NOW can we go and look for Katerina?"
"But it's too late, it's nearly dark," said the mayor.
"We'd better have something to eat at my house
and go and look for Katerina in the morning."
"Then I'll worry about her all night," said Millie.
She was very sad.

There were nice things to eat at the mayor's house
and everyone was happy.
Everyone except Millie.
She thought of Katerina lost out there in the dark.
She thought, "Perhaps I'll never see her again."
She was so sad that she wanted to cry.

She found a place
where no one could see her.
She sat there and cried.
She cried and thought,
"Oh Katerina, where are you?"
And it was just as well
she didn't know
BECAUSE...

Please do not feed the Hippos!

…Katerina had found yet another new pond
and this was the worst of the lot.
"Dive, everybody!" shouted Charlie.
"Dive! Dive! Dive!"

Afterwards the goslings were crying.

"We might all have been eaten," said Charlie.

"I've had enough of your lovely new ponds.

Which way is home?"

"I don't know," said Katerina.

Much, much later she found another way out.

"No!" said Charlie.

"Just one more try," said Katerina.

"No!" said Charlie.

"This one is different," said Katerina. "I know!

I absolutely know that this will take us to a lovely new pond!"

BUT…

In the mayor's bathroom
Millie was tired out with crying.
Suddenly she heard something.
It sounded like a goose.
Then she saw something.

It looked like a goose.
And another goose!
And five goslings!
"Katerina!" she shouted.
"Oh Katerina! You're back!"

Everyone was very surprised to hear where Katerina had been.
"I knew the pipes were all ajumble," said Mr Patel.
"But who'd have thought that geese would climb up
a pipe into the mayor's bathroom?"

"We'd better take them back to the pond," said the mayor.
Everyone wanted to come along.
"I'll drive," said Mr Patel's brother.

"Off you go, Katerina," said the mayor.
"Your pond is all filled up.

You and Charlie and the goslings are safely home.
Now Millie won't need to worry anymore."

And that night Millie did not worry about Katerina.
She had a lovely dream instead.
She was very happy.

Katerina was happy too.
"I told you," she said. "I told you
we'd find a lovely new pond in the end."
"This is not a lovely new pond," said Charlie.
"This is our lovely old pond."
"But with new water," said Katerina.
Then they all went to sleep.